The Movie Storybook

Adapted by Sarah Nathan

Based on the screenplay written by Bill Kelly

Executive Producers Chris Chase, Sunil Perkash, Ezra Swerdlow

Produced by Barry Josephson and Barry Sonnenfeld

Directed by Kevin Lima

Copyright © 2007 by Disney Enterprises, Inc.

All rights reserved. Published by Disney Press, an imprint of Disney Book Group. No part of this book may be reproduced or transmitted in any form or by any means, electronic or mechanical, including photocopying, recording, or by any information storage and retrieval system, without written permission from the publisher. For information address Disney Press, 114 Fifth Avenue, New York, New York 10011-5690.

Printed in the United States of America

First Edition

1 3 5 7 9 10 8 6 4 2

Library of Congress Catalog Card Number on file.

ISBN-13: 978-1-4231-0911-2

ISBN-10: 1-4231-0911-2

DiSNEY PRESS

New York

Once upon a time, in a magical kingdom known as Andalasia, there lived a beautiful young maiden named Giselle. She lived in a tree house in the enchanted forest, surrounded by many animal friends. Giselle's best friend was Pip, a tiny chipmunk with a big heart, who was loyal and true. Giselle was happy, but she longed to meet her one true love.

In another part of the kingdom, there lived a handsome prince named Edward. He was strong and full of charm. To keep the kingdom safe, he spent his days hunting nasty trolls with his valet, Nathaniel, at his side. The prince did not want for anything—except his one true love.

Then, one fateful day, while Edward was out hunting trolls, he began to sing a song about true love's kiss. Suddenly, through the forest, a beautiful voice rang out, as if in answer to his song. Leaping upon his horse, Edward took off after the voice. Whoever could sing such a song was surely meant for him!

He found out who it was soon enough, when Giselle fell into his arms—quite literally—as he saved her from a particularly mean and nasty troll. Edward looked into her lovely eyes and declared, "We shall be married in the morning." Then, as the forest animals looked on, the pair began to sing their own song of true love.

Everyone in the kingdom was happy . . . except for
Edward's evil stepmother, Queen Narissa. If the pair were
to marry, she would no longer be queen. So on their
wedding day, Narissa, disguised as an old woman, tricked
Giselle into a magical wishing well!

Giselle tumbled down a dark tunnel. And as she fell, she
felt the strangest sensation in her arms and legs. What was
happening?

Thump!

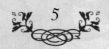

Taking a deep breath, Giselle looked around. All was quiet in the damp, dark place, except for the distant echo of dripping water. The only light came through five small holes in a circle above her head. With all her might, Giselle pushed the circle away and lifted herself up into a new reality—Times Square in New York City!

"Hello! Excuse me! Pardon me!" Giselle called to the
busy New Yorkers who were pushing their way along the
crowded street. "I wonder if one of you kind people might
direct me to the castle?"

People looked at her funny, but did not stop. No one
helped her. Giselle searched all around the large city, but
the castle was nowhere in sight.

To make matters worse, it started to rain. This was not
the way Giselle had envisioned her wedding day!

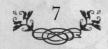

The day grew darker, and the rain kept falling. Giselle was exhausted and drenched from walking in the rain. She was almost out of hope when suddenly she looked up and saw a beautiful castle.

Unfortunately, this castle was a billboard advertisement. But Giselle thought it was real. She leaped on a car, then climbed the ladder leading up to the billboard walkway. The metal surface was slippery from the rain, and Giselle fought to keep her balance.

Close by, a handsome, but rather serious, lawyer named Robert was riding in a taxi with his daughter, Morgan. Morgan believed in fairy tales, even though her practical father always told her that they were not real.

From the backseat of the cab, Morgan looked out her window and gasped. There was a princess on a billboard! She raced out of the cab and called up to the woman.

"Oh, hello!" Giselle exclaimed. "I was wondering if maybe you—" Giselle's foot slid on the wet metal. She slipped and caught hold of the ledge with her hands but she couldn't hold on. Giselle fell!

"Catch her, Daddy!" Morgan cried.

Robert raced forward, reaching up his arms. Giselle dropped into his arms, and together they fell on to the wet pavement.

Thunder boomed and the rain continued to pour down. They had to get out of the storm—and so all three went back to Robert's apartment. On the way, Giselle told Robert and Morgan about Prince Edward and how she had gotten to New York.

"No doubt by morning he'll come and rescue me from this strange land," Giselle said. "He'll take me home and the two of us can share in true love's kiss!"

"True love's kiss?" Robert asked, raising an eyebrow.

Giselle looked at Robert with great sincerity. "It's the most powerful thing in the world."

"Right," Robert said. It was clear—he didn't believe in that kind of power.

At the apartment door, Giselle stopped. The large hoop skirt of her wedding gown was too wide for the opening. Giselle was stuck!

Morgan reached out to help the maiden. With a strong tug, Giselle tumbled into the apartment—though her hoop was still firmly wedged in the door.

After everyone had dried off, Robert pulled out his phone. He was going to call a car for Giselle.

"You're not really gonna make her go, are you Daddy?" Morgan asked.

Robert considered his daughter's plea. He did not like the idea of a stranger sleeping on his couch—but she *had* looked rather sleepy, and it *was* raining out. Then, he glanced over at the couch. Giselle had already fallen asleep.

Sighing, he put away the phone. He would figure out what to do with Giselle in the morning.

The next morning, in busy Times Square, Prince Edward popped out of the very same manhole Giselle had emerged from not too long ago. He had come to rescue his bride-to-be.

Pip had joined him on the quest, and he was prepared to do anything to help his friend Giselle. But when he went to tell Edward that, he couldn't! In this world, all Pip could do was squeak like a regular chipmunk! He grabbed his throat to try and let the prince know of this unfortunate circumstance. But the prince did not understand. He merely thought Pip was speechless in his esteemed presence. "Come along, Pip," Edward said, ignoring the chipmunk's gestures. "We've got a maiden to find."

In another part of the city, Giselle yawned and opened her eyes. She had been so tired the night before that she had barely noticed Robert and Morgan's apartment. But now, in the light of day, she could see it was quite messy. This just would not do. Since her new friends had been so kind to her, she wanted to do something nice for them. She would clean their home.

She rushed to the window and started to sing, calling animals to help with the cleaning. After all, birds, bunnies, and chipmunks were among the best cleaners in the forest. However, Giselle was not in the Andalasian forest anymore. And the creatures who heeded her call were New York City vermin like rats, pigeons, and cockroaches.

Giselle was surprised at the cleaning crew, but she smiled warmly at the creatures. "All right, everyone!" she called. "Let's tidy things up!"

As Giselle and her friends cleaned, Morgan was slowly waking up. Hearing a commotion outside, she went to her bedroom door and pulled it open. Then she let out a gasp. A group of mice was doing the laundry! She ran to get her father. "Wake up!" Morgan yelled, bouncing on her dad's bed. "You have to come see!"

When Robert saw all the vermin in his apartment, he panicked. He and Morgan worked quickly to get rid of the critters. They had just finished clearing the apartment of wildlife when the doorbell rang. It was Nancy—Robert's girlfriend.

Looking around, Nancy's eyes widened. The apartment had never looked so clean. But even more surprising was the redheaded woman in the apartment. Giselle stood there, unaware of the tension her presence was causing.

But Robert was well aware. He watched Nancy grow madder and madder. Then, with a huff, Nancy stormed out of the apartment.

Robert's day wasn't going very well. He woke up to rodents in his house. Nancy was angry with him. And to top it all off, he just realized—Giselle had made a dress out of his living room curtains!

At the same time, not terribly far away, a New York City bus quickly came to a screeching halt. Prince Edward had just pierced his sword through the roof! Now, he swung down and peered in through the open door.

"Giselle? My love?" he called. Then he regarded the busload of New Yorkers. "The steel beast is dead, peasants! I set you all free!"

The driver leaped out of the bus, furious. No one stopped her on her route!

Luckily for Edward, Nathaniel had just arrived in Manhattan as well and he managed to save the prince from the mean driver. But helping Edward was not Nathaniel's true purpose. Narissa had sent him to stop the prince from finding Giselle. He would do whatever it took to make his beloved queen happy.

A short while later, Nathaniel found himself in the kitchen of a New York City restaurant. He was there to secretly contact Narissa. Suddenly, the queen's voice boomed through the room. She was staring at him from a pot of boiling water!

Narissa sent the bumbling Nathaniel three poisoned apples. "Just one bite," she hissed. "That's all it takes." Then, Giselle would never be a problem again.

Unfortunately for Nathaniel, Pip overheard everything and raced out to warn Prince Edward. Unable to speak, he tried to act out his message, but the prince did not understand. "You feel you'd die without me near?" Edward asked.

Pip sighed. It seemed he would have to save Giselle from the queen *and* Nathaniel all by himself. This was a very tall order for such a tiny chipmunk!

While Nathaniel was plotting with Narissa, Robert had to deal with his own headache. Giselle kept getting him into trouble! First she had messed things up with Nancy, and then she almost got him fired from his job!

Robert was a divorce lawyer—it was his business to help people separate. But when Giselle had discovered that one of Robert's clients was getting a divorce, she had started to cry. She could not understand why two people would not want to be together forever. When his boss walked in and saw Giselle crying over lost love, it was not good for Robert.

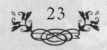

So Robert had made up his mind. While she was beautiful and charming in her own naïve way, Giselle was too much trouble. She had to go home. Leaving his office, he walked her toward the entrance to Central Park.

"Here's some money," he said gently. "I want you to take it and call your prince." Then, he said his good-byes and began to walk back to the office. But before he got very far, Giselle found trouble—again. She was giving her money away to an old woman!

Worried, Robert rushed over and pulled Giselle away. Then, as they strolled through the park, they began to talk. "How long have you known your prince?" Robert asked as they walked down a tree-lined path.

"Oh," Giselle said, "about a day."

Robert was shocked. He and Nancy had been going on dates for five years. When he told Giselle that, she looked confused. "Date?" she asked.

"Yeah, a date! You go someplace special," he explained. Then he added that dating was a good way to get to know a person *before* you got married.

As they were talking, Nathaniel, in disguise, came up to Giselle and offered her a caramel apple. But this was no ordinary apple—it was one of Narissa's poisoned apples! Just as she was about to take a bite, Giselle made a sudden gesture and the apple flew out of her hand. She was safe—for now.

As they continued to walk along, Robert began to enjoy himself. Giselle was charming and fun to be with. That is, until she began to sing! Robert's face grew red with embarrassment—everyone was staring! And soon, more and more people were joining in. Musicians picked up the tune and dancers moved along to the melody. It was hard not to get swept up in Giselle's song and dance.

Pausing, Giselle whistled and two doves flew onto her outstretched hand. She gave them a bouquet of flowers, and asked that they deliver the flowers to Nancy.

Moments later, Nancy called Robert on his cell phone. She had gotten the flowers, and she loved them! Robert left to go meet Nancy. But before he did, he glanced at Giselle. How had she done that?

Later that evening, Robert, Giselle, and Morgan went out to dinner. Nathaniel, who was keeping a careful watch over Giselle, was at the restaurant disguised as a waiter. He offered Giselle a special drink made from another poisoned apple. Luckily, Pip was there to prevent Giselle from drinking the potion.

Pip's presence did not go unnoticed by the customers in the restaurant. As the chipmunk frantically gestured about the poisoned apple drink, people thought that the little animal was attacking Giselle. But Giselle did not care. Pip had told her the most wonderful news—Edward was in the city and he was looking for her!

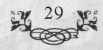

When the sun rose in the sky the next morning, Giselle was already up. She was wearing a new dress made from the curtains in Morgan's bedroom and making breakfast. Suddenly, the doorbell rang. Giselle looked at Robert and Morgan—who could it be?

"I've come to rescue my lovely bride, the fair Giselle!" Prince Edward declared, striding into the apartment. When he saw Robert, the prince stopped and flashed his sword. He thought that Robert had been holding Giselle captive and was prepared to fight him.

Giselle did not want the two men to fight. Quickly, she introduced everyone. When Edward was sure that Robert had not kidnapped his true love, he put away his sword. Then, he began to sing to Giselle.

For a few moments, the apartment was filled with the sound of his voice. But he trailed off as he realized he was singing alone. Giselle had not joined him. She was too busy thinking.

"Before we leave," she said, "there's one thing I would love to do."

"Name it, my love," Edward answered, "and it is done."

Giselle asked Edward if they could go on a date. Even though the prince had not heard of such a thing, he readily agreed.

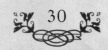

When it was time for Giselle to say good-bye to her
new friends, she realized that she was not as happy about
leaving as she would have imagined.

Nevertheless, a short while later, Giselle found herself
on the Brooklyn Bridge with her prince. As they walked
down the path, she tried not to think about Robert or
Morgan, even though she wanted to see them again.

Then, she had an idea. There was a ball later that night. Robert and Nancy were going to attend, so why shouldn't Giselle and Edward?

Edward agreed to go, and so Giselle raced back to Robert's apartment to find Morgan. At such short notice, she would need a fairy godmother to help her get ready! "I have something better than a fairy godmother," the little girl said. She had a credit card! It was only supposed to be used for emergencies—but a princess without a dress the day of a ball was certainly an emergency!

Morgan took Giselle to the nicest shops in New York City. A girl going to a ball needed many new things, and Morgan knew just what to buy—a dress and slippers (glass, of course!). After hours of shopping, the two settled into a salon for a beauty treatment worthy of two princesses. Morgan was truly happy. Being with Giselle was a dream come true. "So is this what it's like?" Morgan asked.

"What, sweetie?" Giselle asked.

"Going shopping with your mother," Morgan said.

Giselle had never been shopping with her mother. She confessed to Morgan that she didn't know. "But I like it," Giselle added.

"Me, too," Morgan said.

When Giselle and Prince Edward arrived at the ball later
that evening, Giselle could not believe her eyes. It was a
costume ball! The guests were dressed in traditional fairy-
tale outfits. She felt totally out of place in her sophisticated
gown. Then she saw Robert and her heart began to beat
faster. How had she not noticed how handsome he was
before? He looked like a prince!

And he thought she looked like a princess. As the band
began to play a new song, the bandleader instructed the
crowd to dance with somebody other than their own date.
Prince Edward took Nancy's hand, and Robert escorted
Giselle to the dance floor.

Robert guided Giselle around the ballroom in a waltz. Giselle felt like she was floating on air. She sighed and rested her head against his shoulder, enjoying the perfect moment. And then Nancy came back for her partner.

Giselle watched Robert twirl away with Nancy, and her heart ached. She did not belong in this world—or with Robert. With sadness in her heart, she told Prince Edward she was ready to go home. While he dashed off to get her wrap, an old woman appeared at Giselle's side.

It was Narissa! Disguised as the old woman who had tricked Giselle back in Andalasia, she held out an apple to Giselle. "Just one bite, my love," Narissa said, "and all this will go away."

Giselle glanced over at the dance floor to see Robert and Nancy dancing. Her eyes filled with tears, she lifted the apple to her lips and took a bite.

A thunderbolt struck as Giselle fell to the floor. The apple rolled from her hand, down the large staircase and landed by Robert's foot. As he picked the fruit up, Narissa's evil cackle filled the room.

Meanwhile, Prince Edward returned to find his stepmother dragging Giselle away. He called out for help. Robert and Nancy quickly ran to see what had happened.

Just then, Nathaniel and Pip arrived. Nathaniel had grown tired of doing the queen's evil work. He confessed Narissa's plan. "She poisoned her!" Nathaniel shouted.

No one knew what to do. The clock in the hall started to chime. "When the clock strikes twelve," Narissa said, "she'll be dead!"

Hearing Narissa's words, Robert's heart stopped. He couldn't let Giselle die. Suddenly, he had an idea. "True love's kiss . . ." he said. "It's the most powerful thing in the world."

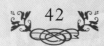

Edward heard Robert and sprang into action. He rushed
to Giselle's side and gave her a kiss. Giselle didn't move.
Prince Edward glanced over at Robert as the clock chimed
again. Perhaps the kiss wasn't from the right man?

Robert shook his head. "It's not possible," he said. "It
couldn't be me!"

"It has to be," Prince Edward said.

With a nod from Nancy, Robert leaned over at the
stroke of midnight and gently kissed Giselle. Everyone
leaned in to watch, anxious to see if Giselle would wake up.
Slowly, Giselle opened her eyes. She gazed at Robert. "I
knew it was you," she said with a smile.

"Noooooooooooo!!!" screamed Narissa. This was not part of her plan! Chanting some magical words, Narissa caused a burst of energy that knocked out Edward and Nathaniel. Then she began to transform into a giant, scaly beast with a long tail and sharp claws. She reached for Giselle, but Robert gallantly stood in Narissa's way. "Over my dead body," he said.

"All right. I'm flexible," Narissa said. Then, she snatched up Robert and ran out of the ballroom.

Grabbing Prince Edward's sword, Giselle kicked off her glass slippers and took off after them. She was going to save her true love.

Outside on the roof, the Narissa beast dangled Robert over the edge of the tall building. "Narissa!" Giselle yelled. "I am not going to let you take him!"

Narissa ignored Giselle and continued to climb up onto the tall spire of the building. Giselle followed. At that moment, Pip arrived and jumped on the Narissa beast's head. The tiny bit of extra weight was just enough to knock the beast off balance.

As Narissa toppled off the building, Giselle hurled the sword with all her strength, pinning Robert's sleeve to the spire. For a moment, Robert seemed to be safe.

Then, he began to slip.

"Hold on!" Giselle shouted. But it was too late—Robert was falling . . . right into the waiting arms of Giselle.

And there, high above the city, Robert and Giselle shared another kiss of true love.

Soon after, Robert and Giselle were married. They started Andalasia Fashions, where they made princess dresses for children, and Morgan's dreams of having a family came true.

Prince Edward and Nancy wound up being a perfect match and were married in Andalasia. And both Pip and Nathaniel wrote best-selling books about their enchanting adventures.

True love's kiss had sealed their fates and filled their hearts with joy.

And they *all* lived happily ever after.